C000302643

Xingu: A Short Story
Includes The Vice of Reading
and a Reading Discussion Guide

Edith Wharton

Ordinary Matters Publishing

HOUSTON, TEXAS USA

Copyright © 2014 by **Vikk Simmons**
Xingu by Edith Wharton (1915)
A Vice of Reading by Edith Wharton (1903)
Foreword and Reading Discussion Guide by Vikk Simmons (2014)

All rights reserved. No part of this publication may be reproduced, distributed or transmitted in any form or by any means, without prior written permission.

Ordinary Matters Publishing
PO Box 430577
Houston, Texas USA 77243
www.ordinarymatterspublishing.com

Publisher's Note: Xingu is a work of fiction. Names, characters, places, and incidents are a product of the author's imagination. Locales and public names are sometimes used for atmospheric purposes. Any resemblance to actual people, living or dead, or to businesses, companies, events, institutions, or locales is completely coincidental.

Cover and Interior Images: Public Domain

Miss Lily Else, 11539 D Rotary Photo, E.C. (Circa 1909)
Edith Wharton 1870 painted by Edward Harrison May (Photographer Flickr Cliff1066 via Wikimendia Commons)
Edith Wharton with dog, Roseti, Public Domain

Cover Design by Peter Arnott
Book Layout © 2014 BookDesignTemplates.com

Xingu: A Short Story/ Edith Wharton (Guide). -- 1st ed.
ISBN 978-1-941303-03-0
Printed in the United States of America

Publishing history (Public Domain)
Xingu by Edith Wharton/Scribner's Magazine, December 1915
The Vice of Reading by Edith Wharton/North American Review 177, October, 1903

To my parents, who demonstrated
their love of reading every single day.

"A classic is classic not because it conforms to certain
structural rules, or fits certain definitions (of which its
author had quite probably never heard). It is classic
because of a certain and irrepressible freshness."

—EDITH WHARTON

Contents

Foreword

Want a fast, fun read? Read Xingu. I love short stories, and Edith Wharton's short story Xingu has become a favorite. I stumbled across this gem a few years ago in preparation for a 24-hour readathon and have been recommending the story ever since to anyone who will listen. Downtown Abbey fans should really enjoy this particular Wharton story.

Wharton is witty and sharp. Her story is great for anyone who loves books, participates in book clubs, or is simply in the mood for a good read that is also a quick, lighthearted romp. Wharton uses her literary skills to tease and play with the reader as much as she does with the cast of characters.

In addition to the full text of *Xingu*, you will also find:

- The full text of Wharton's essay *The Vice of Reading*
- Discussion questions for readers or book clubs
- Quotes from *Xingu*
- A link to the audio version of Xingu
- More information about Edith Wharton
- A complete list of Wharton's short stories
- Information on the Short Works Reading Challenge

Since my first reading of Xingu, I've realized that Wharton is a great writer for today's modern reader. She's as relevant now as she was in her own day. Wharton understands peer pressure, societal pressures, and a consumer-based society whose main focus is to feed from the renewable trough. Despite her writing at the turn of the 20th century, she is definitely a writer for the 21st.

Xingu is a great introduction to Edith Wharton and her work. I've added a reader's guide with a little back story and discussion questions as an added bonus. When I discovered Wharton's essay *The Vice of Reading*, I realized how much *Xingu* reflected the thoughts found in the essay. Those who would like to learn more about Wharton's attitudes about readers and the act of reading can do so by reading the included essay.

Leisurely reading isn't much of an option for many, so reading short stories is a viable alternative for today's readers. You can read short stories in fifteen or thirty minutes, most within an hour. Why not carve out time for to read some short works? I've provided a list of Wharton's many short stories, but you'll discover soon enough that short stories are a favorite form of many writers, both old and new.

Be sure and check out The Short Works Reading Challenge.

SHORT WORKS READING CHALLENGE
http://www.DownTheWritersPath.com/short-stories-challenge

For your free copy of *Why Writers Keep Journals* go to:

CoffeeBreakJournals.com

Now it's time to join Mrs. Ballinger and the other Lunch Club ladies dubbed "huntresses of erudition" for a rather surprising literary discussion about Xingu.

Vikk Simmons, 2014

Note: The audio version link is provided at the end of the discussion questions.

Roseti

297 FIFTH AVE, N.Y.

Vikk Simmons

Xingu

Part 1

Mrs. Ballinger is one of the ladies who pursue Culture in bands, as though it were dangerous to meet alone. To this end she had founded the Lunch Club, an association composed of herself and several other indomitable huntresses of erudition. The Lunch Club, after three or four winters of lunching and debate, had acquired such local distinction that the entertainment of distinguished strangers became one of its accepted functions; in recognition of which it duly extended to the celebrated "Osric Dane," on the day of her arrival in Hillbridge, an invitation to be present at the next meeting.

The club was to meet at Mrs. Ballinger's. The other members, behind her back, were of one voice in deploring her unwillingness to cede her rights in favor of Mrs. Plinth, whose house made a more impressive setting for the entertainment of celebrities; while, as Mrs. Leveret observed, there was always the picture-gallery to fall back on.

Mrs. Plinth made no secret of sharing this view. She had always regarded it as one of her obligations to entertain the Lunch Club's distinguished guests. Mrs. Plinth was almost as proud of her obligations as she was of her picture-gallery. She was in fact fond of implying that the one possession implied the other, and that only a woman of her wealth could afford to live up to a standard as high as that which she had set herself. An all-round sense of duty, roughly adaptable to various ends, was, in her opinion, all that Providence exacted of the more humbly stationed; but the power which had predestined Mrs. Plinth to keep a footman clearly intended her to maintain an equally specialized staff of responsibilities. It was the more to be regretted that Mrs. Ballinger, whose obligations to society were bounded by the narrow scope of two parlour-maids, should have been so tenacious of the right to entertain Osric Dane.

The question of that lady's reception had for a month past profoundly moved the members of the Lunch Club. It was not that they felt themselves unequal to the task, but that their sense of the opportunity plunged them into the agreeable uncertainty of the lady who weighs the alternatives of a well-stocked wardrobe. If such subsidiary members as Mrs. Leveret were fluttered by the thought of exchanging ideas with the author of "The Wings of Death," no forebodings disturbed the conscious adequacy of Mrs. Plinth, Mrs. Ballinger, and Miss Van Vluyck. "The Wings of Death" had, in fact, at Miss Van Vluyck's suggestion, been chosen as the subject of discussion at the last club meeting, and each member had thus been enabled to express her own opinion or to appropriate whatever sounded well in the comments of the others.

Mrs. Roby alone had abstained from profiting by the opportunity, but it was now openly recognised that, as a member of the Lunch Club, Mrs. Roby was a failure. "It all comes," as Miss Van Vluyck put it, "of accepting a woman on a man's estimation." Mrs. Roby, returning to Hillbridge from a prolonged sojourn in exotic lands--the other ladies no longer took the trouble to remember where--had been heralded by the distinguished biologist, Professor Foreland, as the most agreeable woman he had ever met; and the members of the Lunch Club, impressed by an encomium that carried the weight of a diploma, and rashly assuming that the Professor's social sympathies would follow the line of his professional bent, had seized the chance of annexing a biological member. Their disillusionment was complete. At Miss Van Vluyck's first off-hand mention of the pterodactyl Mrs. Roby had confusedly murmured: "I know so little about *metres*--" and after that painful betrayal of incompetence she had prudently withdrawn from farther participation in the mental gymnastics of the club.

"I suppose she flattered him," Miss Van Vluyck summed up," or else it's the way she does her hair."

The dimensions of Miss Van Vluyck's dining-room having restricted the membership of the club to six, the nonconductiveness of one member was a serious obstacle to the exchange of ideas, and some wonder had already been expressed that Mrs. Roby should care to live, as it were, on the intellectual bounty of the others. This feeling was increased by the discovery that she had not yet read "The Wings of Death." She owned to having heard the name of Osric Dane, but that-- incredible as it appeared--was the extent of her acquaintance with the celebrated novelist. The ladies could not conceal their surprise, but Mrs. Ballinger, whose pride in the club made her wish to put even Mrs. Roby in the best possible light, gently insinuated that, though she had not had time to acquaint herself with "The Wings of Death," she must at least be familiar with its equally remarkable predecessor, "The Supreme Instant."

Mrs. Roby wrinkled her sunny brows in a conscientious effort of memory, as a result of which she recalled that, oh, yes, she *had* seen the book at her brother's, when she was staying with him in Brazil, and had even carried it off to read one day on a boating party; but they had all got to shying things at each other in the boat, and the book had gone overboard, so she had never had the chance--

The picture evoked by this anecdote did not increase Mrs. Roby's credit with the club, and there was a painful pause, which was broken by Mrs. Plinth's remarking: "I can understand that, with all your other pursuits, you should not find much time for reading; but I should have thought you might at least have *got up* 'The Wings of Death' before Osric Dane's arrival."

Mrs. Roby took this rebuke good-humouredly. She had meant, she owned, to glance through the book; but she had been so absorbed in a novel of Trollope's that--

"No one reads Trollope now," Mrs. Ballinger interrupted.

Mrs. Roby looked pained. "I'm only just beginning," she confessed.

"And does he interest you?" Mrs. Plinth enquired.

"He amuses me."

"Amusement," said Mrs. Plinth, "is hardly what I look for in my choice of books."

"Oh, certainly, 'The Wings of Death' is not amusing," ventured Mrs. Leveret, whose manner of putting forth an opinion was like that of an obliging salesman with a variety of other styles to submit if his first selection does not suit.

"Was it *meant* to be?" enquired Mrs. Plinth, who was fond of asking questions that she permitted no one but herself to answer. "Assuredly not."

"Assuredly not--that is what I was going to say," assented Mrs. Leveret, hastily rolling up her opinion and reaching for another. "It was meant to--to elevate."

Miss Van Vluyck adjusted her spectacles as though they were the black cap of condemnation. "I hardly see," she interposed, "how a book steeped in the bitterest pessimism can be said to elevate however much it may instruct."

"I meant, of course, to instruct," said Mrs. Leveret, flurried by the unexpected distinction between two terms which she had supposed to be synonymous. Mrs. Leveret's enjoyment of the Lunch Club was frequently marred by such surprises; and not knowing her own value to the other ladies as a mirror for their mental complacency, she was sometimes troubled by a doubt of her worthiness to join in their debates. It was only the fact of having a dull sister who thought her clever that saved her, from a sense of hopeless inferiority.

"Do they get married in the end?" Mrs. Roby interposed.

"They--who?" the Lunch Club collectively exclaimed.

"Why, the girl and man. It's a novel, isn't it? I always think that's the one thing that matters. If they're parted, it spoils my dinner."

Mrs. Plinth and Mrs. Ballinger exchanged scandalised glances, and the latter said: "I should hardly advise you to read 'The Wings of Death' in that spirit. For my part, when there are so many books one *has* to read; I wonder how any one can find time for those that are merely amusing."

"The beautiful part of it," Laura Glyde murmured, "is surely just this--that no one can tell how 'The Wings of Death' ends. Osric Dane, overcome by the awful significance of her own meaning, has mercifully veiled it--perhaps even from herself--as Apelles, in representing the sacrifice of Iphigenia, veiled the face or Agamemnon."

"What's that? Is it poetry?" whispered Mrs. Leveret to Mrs. Plinth, who, disdaining a definite reply, said coldly: "You should look it up. I always make it a point to look things up." Her tone added--"though I might easily have it done for me by the footman."

"I was about to say," Miss Van Vluyck resumed, "that it must always be a question whether a book *can* instruct unless it elevates."

"Oh--" murmured Mrs. Leveret, now feeling herself hopelessly astray.

"I don't know," said Mrs. Ballinger, scenting in Miss Van Vluyck's tone a tendency to depreciate the coveted distinction of entertaining Osric Dane; "I don't know that such a question can seriously be raised as to a book which has attracted more attention among thoughtful people than any novel since 'Robert Elsmere.'"

"Oh, but don't you see," exclaimed Laura Glyde, "that it's just the dark hopelessness of it all--the wonderful tone-scheme of black on black--that makes it such an artistic achievement? It reminded me when I read it of Prince Rupert's *manière noire*...the book is etched, not painted, yet one feels the colour-values so intensely. . ."

"Who is *he*?" Mrs. Leveret whispered to her neighbour. "Some one she's met abroad?"

"The wonderful part of the book," Mrs. Ballinger conceded, "is that it may be looked at from so many points of view. I hear that as a study of determinism, Professor Lupton ranks it with 'The Data of Ethics.'"

"I'm told that Osric Dane spent ten years in preparatory studies before beginning to write it," said Mrs. Plinth. "She looks up everything--verifies everything. It has always been my principle, as you know. Nothing would induce me, now, to put aside a book before I'd finished it, just because I can buy as many more as I want."

"And what do *you* think of 'The Wings of Death'?" Mrs. Roby abruptly asked her.

It was the kind of question that might be termed out of order, and the ladies glanced at each other as though disclaiming any share in such a breach of discipline. They all knew there was nothing Mrs. Plinth so much disliked as being asked her opinion of a book. Books were written to read; if one read them what more could be expected? To be questioned in detail regarding the contents of a volume seemed to her as great an outrage as being searched for smuggled laces at the Custom House. The club had always respected this idiosyncrasy of Mrs. Plinth's. Such opinions as she had were imposing and substantial: her mind, like her house, was furnished with monumental "pieces" that were not meant to be disarranged; and it was one of the unwritten rules of the Lunch Club that, within her own province, each member's habits of thought should be respected. The meeting therefore closed with an increased sense, on the part of the other ladies, of Mrs. Roby's hopeless unfitness to be one of them.

Vikk Simmons

Part 2

Mrs. Leveret, on the eventful day, arrived early at Mrs. Ballinger's, her volume of *Appropriate Allusions* in her pocket.

It always flustered Mrs. Leveret to be late at the Lunch Club: she liked to collect her thoughts and gather a hint, as the others assembled, of the turn the conversation was likely to take. To-day, however, she felt herself completely at a loss; and even the familiar contact of *Appropriate Allusions*, which stuck into her as she sat down, failed to give her any reassurance. It was an admirable little volume, compiled to meet all the social emergencies; so that, whether on the occasion of Anniversaries, joyful or melancholy (as the classification ran), of Banquets, social or municipal, or of Baptisms, Church of England or sectarian, its student need never be at a loss for a pertinent reference. Mrs. Leveret, though she had for years devoutly conned its pages, valued it, however, rather for its moral support than for its practical services; for though in the privacy of her own room she commanded an army of quotations, these invariably deserted her at the critical moment, and the only phrase she retained--*Canst thou draw out leviathan with a hook?*--was one she had never yet found occasion to apply.

To-day she felt that even the complete mastery of the volume would hardly have insured her self-possession; for she thought it probable that, even if she *did*, in some miraculous way, remember an Allusion, it would be only to find that Osric Dane used a different volume (Mrs. Leveret was convinced that literary people always carried them), and would consequently not recognise her quotations.

Mrs. Leveret's sense of being adrift was intensified by the appearance of Mrs. Ballinger's drawing room. To a careless eye, its aspect was unchanged; but those acquainted with Mrs.

Ballinger's way of arranging her books would instantly have detected the marks of recent perturbation. Mrs. Ballinger's province, as a member of the Lunch Club, was the Book of the Day. On that, whatever it was, from a novel to a treatise on experimental psychology, she was confidently, authoritatively "up." What became of last year's books, or last week's even; what she did with the "subjects" she had previously professed with equal authority; no one had ever yet discovered. 'Her mind was a hotel where facts came and went like transient lodgers, without leaving their address behind, and frequently without paying for their board.' It was Mrs. Ballinger's boast that she was "abreast with the Thought of the Day," and her pride that this advanced position should be expressed by the books on her table. These volumes, frequently renewed, and almost always damp from the press, bore names generally unfamiliar to Mrs. Leveret, and giving her, as she furtively scanned them, a disheartening glimpse of new fields of knowledge to be breathlessly traversed in Mrs. Ballinger's wake. But to-day a number of maturer-looking volumes were adroitly mingled with the *primeurs* of the press--Karl Marx jostled Professor Bergson, and the "Confessions of St. Augustine" lay beside the last work on "Mendelism;" so that even to Mrs. Leveret's fluttered perceptions it was clear that Mrs. Ballinger didn't in the least know what Osric Dane was likely to talk about, and had taken measures to be prepared for anything. Mrs. Leveret felt like a passenger on an ocean steamer who is told that there is no immediate danger, but that she had better put on her life-belt.

It was a relief to be roused from these forebodings by Miss Van Vluyck's arrival.

"Well, my dear," the new-comer briskly asked her hostess, "what subjects are we to discuss to-day?"

Mrs. Ballinger was furtively replacing a volume of Words-worth by a copy of Verlaine. "I hardly know," she said, somewhat nervously. "Perhaps we had better leave that to circumstances."

"Circumstances?" said Miss Van Vluyck drily. "That means, I suppose, that Laura Glyde will take the floor as usual, and we shall be deluged with literature."

Philanthropy and statistics were Miss Van Vluyck's province, and she resented any tendency to divert their guest's attention from these topics.

Mrs. Plinth at this moment appeared.

"Literature?" she protested in a tone of remonstrance. "But this is perfectly unexpected. I understood we were to talk of Osric Dane's novel."

Mrs. Ballinger winced at the discrimination, but let it pass. "We can hardly make that our chief subject--at least not *too* intentionally," she suggested. "Of course we can let our talk *drift* in that direction; but we ought to have some other topic as an introduction, and that is what I wanted to consult you about. The fact is, we know so little of Osric Dane's tastes and interests that it is difficult to make any special preparation."

"It may be difficult," said Mrs. Plinth with decision, "but it is necessary. I know what that happy-go-lucky principle leads to. As I told one of my nieces the other day, there are certain emergencies for which a lady should always be prepared. It's in shocking taste to wear colours when one pays a visit of condolence, or a last year's dress when there are reports that one's husband is on the wrong side of the market, and so it is with conversation. All I ask is that I should know beforehand what is to be talked about; then I feel sure of being able to say the proper thing."

"I quite agree with you," Mrs. Ballinger assented; "but--"

And at that instant, heralded by the fluttered parlourmaid, Osric Dane appeared upon the threshold.

Mrs. Leveret told her sister afterward that she had known at a glance what was coming. She saw that Osric Dane was not going to meet them half way. That distinguished personage had indeed entered with an air of compulsion not calculated to promote the easy exercise of hospitality. She looked as though she were about to be photographed for a new edition of her books.

The desire to propitiate a divinity is generally an inverse ratio to its responsiveness, and the sense of discouragement produced by Osric Dane's entrance visibly increased the Lunch Club's eagerness to please her. Any lingering idea that she might consider herself under an obligation to her entertainers was at once dispelled by her manner. Mrs. Leveret said afterward to her sister, she had a way of looking at you that made you feel as if there was something wrong with your hat. This evidence of greatness produced such an immediate impression on the ladies that a shudder of awe ran through them when Mrs. Roby, as their hostess led the great personage into the dining-room, turned back to whisper to the others: "What a brute she is!"

The hour about the table did not tend to revise this verdict. It was passed by Osric Dane in the silent deglutition of Mrs. Bollinger's menu, and by the members of the club in the emission of tentative platitudes which their guest seemed to swallow as perfunctorily as the successive courses of the luncheon.

Mrs. Ballinger's reluctance to fix a topic had thrown the club into a mental disarray which increased with the return to the drawing-room, where the actual business of discussion was to open. Each lady waited for the other to speak. There was a general shock of disappointment when their hostess opened the conversation by the painfully commonplace enquiry. "Is this your first visit to Hillbridge?"

Even Mrs. Leveret was conscious that this was a bad beginning; and a vague impulse of deprecation made Miss Glyde interject: "It is a very small place indeed."

Mrs. Plinth bristled. "We have a great many representative people," she said, in the tone of one who speaks for her order.

Osric Dane turned to her. "What do they represent?" she asked.

Mrs. Plinth's constitutional dislike to being questioned was intensified by her sense of unpreparedness; and her reproachful glance passed the question on to Mrs. Ballinger.

"Why," said that lady, glancing in turn at the other members, "as a community I hope it is not too much to say that we stand for culture."

"For art--" Miss Glyde interjected.

"For art and literature," Mrs. Ballinger emended.

"And for sociology, I trust," snapped Miss Van Vluyck.

"We have a standard," said Mrs. Plinth, feeling herself suddenly secure on the vast expanse of a generalisation; and Mrs. Leveret, thinking there must be room for more than one on so broad a statement, took courage to murmur: "Oh, certainly; we have a standard."

"The object of our little club," Mrs. Ballinger continued, "is to concentrate the highest tendencies of Hillbridge--to centralise and focus its intellectual effort."

This was felt to be so happy that the ladies drew an almost audible breath of relief.

"We aspire," the President went on, "to be in touch with whatever is highest in art, literature and ethics."

Osric Dane again turned to her. "What ethics?" she asked.

A tremor of apprehension encircled the room. None of the ladies required any preparation to pronounce on a question of morals; but when they were called ethics it was different. The club, when fresh from the "Encyclopaedia Britannica," the "Reader's Handbook" or Smith's "Classical Dictionary," could deal confidently with any subject; but when taken unawares it had been known to define agnosticism as a heresy of the Early Church and Professor Froude as a distinguished histologist; and such minor members as Mrs. Leveret still secretly regarded ethics as something vaguely pagan.

Even to Mrs. Ballinger, Osric Dane's question was unsettling, and there was a general sense of gratitude when Laura Glyde leaned forward to say, with her most sympathetic accent: "You must excuse us, Mrs. Dane, for not being able, just at present, to talk of anything but 'The Wings of Death.'"

"Yes," said Miss Van Vluyck, with a sudden resolve to carry the war into the enemy's camp. "We are so anxious to know the exact purpose you had in mind in writing your wonderful book."

"You will find," Mrs. Plinth interposed, "that we are not superficial readers."

"We are eager to hear from you," Miss Van Vluyck continued, "if the pessimistic tendency of the book is an expression of your own convictions or--"

"Or merely," Miss Glyde thrust in, "a sombre background brushed in to throw your figures into more vivid relief. *Are* you not primarily plastic?"

"I have always maintained," Mrs. Ballinger interposed, "that you represent the purely objective method--"

Osric Dane helped herself critically to coffee. "How do you define objective?" she then enquired.

There was a flurried pause before Laura Glyde intensely murmured: "In reading *you* we don't define, we feel."

Otsric Dane smiled. "The cerebellum," she remarked, "is not infrequently the seat of the literary emotions." And she took a second lump of sugar.

The sting that this remark was vaguely felt to conceal was almost neutralised by the satisfaction of being addressed in such technical language.

"Ah, the cerebellum," said Miss Van Vluyck complacently. "The club took a course in psychology last winter."

"Which psychology?" asked Osric Dane.

There was an agonising pause, during which each member of the club secretly deplored the distressing inefficiency of the others. Only Mrs. Roby went on placidly sipping her chartreuse. At last Mrs. Ballinger said, with an attempt at a high tone: "Well, really, you know, it was last year that we took psychology, and this winter we have been so absorbed in--"

She broke off, nervously trying to recall some of the club's discussions; but her faculties seemed to be paralysed by the petrifying stare of Osric Dane. What *had* the club been absorbed in? Mrs. Ballinger, with a vague purpose of gaining time, repeated slowly: "We've been so intensely absorbed in--"

Mrs. Roby put down her liqueur glass and drew near the group with a smile.

"In Xingu?" she gently prompted.

A thrill ran through the other members. They exchanged confused glances, and then, with one accord, turned a gaze of mingled relief and interrogation on their rescuer. The expression of each denoted a different phase of the same emotion. Mrs. Plinth was the first to compose her features to an air of reassurance: after a moment's hasty adjustment her look almost implied that it was she who had given the word to Mrs. Ballinger.

"Xingu, of course!" exclaimed the latter with her accustomed promptness, while Miss Van Vluyck and Laura Glyde seemed to be plumbing the depths of memory, and Mrs. Leveret, feeling apprehensively for *Appropriate Allusions*, was somehow reassured by the uncomfortable pressure of its bulk against her person.

Osric Dane's change of countenance was no less striking than that of her entertainers. She too put down her coffee-cup, but with a look of distinct annoyance; she too wore, for a brief moment, what Mrs. Roby afterward described as the look of feeling for something in the back of her head; and before she could dissemble these momentary signs of weakness, Mrs. Roby, turning to her with a deferential smile, had said:

"And we've been so hoping that to-day you would tell us just what you think of it."

Osric Dane received the homage of the smile as a matter of course; but the accompanying question obviously embarrassed her, and it became clear to her observers that she was not quick at shifting her facial scenery. It was as though her countenance had so long been set in an expression of unchallenged superiority that the muscles had stiffened, and refused to obey her orders.

"Xingu--" she said, as if seeking in her turn to gain time.

Mrs. Roby continued to press her. "Knowing how engrossing the subject is, you will understand how it happens that the club has let everything else go to the wall for the moment. Since we took up Xingu I might almost say--were it not for your books-- that nothing else seems to us worth remembering."

Osric Dane's stern features were darkened rather than lit up by an uneasy smile. "I am glad to hear that you make one exception," she gave out between narrowed lips.

"Oh, of course," Mrs. Roby said prettily; "but as you have shown us that--so very naturally!--you don't care to talk of your own things, we really can't let you off from telling us exactly what you think about Xingu; especially," she added, with a still more persuasive smile, "as some people say that one of your last books was saturated with it."

It was an *it*, then--the assurance sped like fire through the parched minds of the other members. In their eagerness to gain the least little clue to Xingu they almost forgot the joy of assisting at the discomfiture of Mrs. Dane.

The latter reddened nervously under her antagonist's challenge. "May I ask," she faltered out, "to which of my books you refer?"

Mrs. Roby did not falter. "That's just what I want you to tell us; because, though I was present, I didn't actually take part."

"Present at what?" Mrs. Dane took her up; and for an instant the trembling members of the Lunch Club thought that the champion Providence had raised up for them had lost a point. But Mrs. Roby explained herself gaily: "At the discussion, of course. And so we're dreadfully anxious to know just how it was that you went into the Xingu."

There was a portentous pause, a silence so big with incalculable dangers that the members with one accord checked the words on their lips, like soldiers dropping their arms to watch a single combat between their leaders. Then Mrs. Dane gave expression to their inmost dread by saying sharply: "Ah--you say *the* Xingu, do you?"

Mrs. Roby smiled undauntedly. "It is a shade pedantic, isn't it? Personally, I always drop the article; but I don't know how the other members feel about it."

The other members looked as though they would willingly have dispensed with this appeal to their opinion, and Mrs.

Roby, after a bright glance about the group, went on: "They probably think, as I do, that nothing really matters except the thing itself--except Xingu."

No immediate reply seemed to occur to Mrs. Dane, and Mrs. Ballinger gathered courage to say: "Surely every one must feel that about Xingu."

Mrs. Plinth came to her support with a heavy murmur of assent, and Laura Glyde sighed out emotionally: "I have known cases where it has changed a whole life."

"It has done me worlds of good," Mrs. Leveret interjected, seeming to herself to remember that she had either taken it or read it the winter before.

"Of course," Mrs. Roby admitted, "the difficulty is that one must give up so much time to it. It's very long."

"I can't imagine," said Miss Van Vluyck, "grudging the time given to such a subject."

"And deep in places," Mrs. Roby pursued; (so then it was a book!) "And it isn't easy to skip."

"I never skip," said Mrs. Plinth dogmatically.

"Ah, it's dangerous to, in Xingu. Even at the start there are places where one can't. One must just wade through."

"I should hardly call it *wading*," said Mrs. Ballinger sarcastically.

Mrs. Roby sent her a look of interest. "Ah--you always found it went swimmingly?"

Mrs. Ballinger hesitated. "Of course there are difficult passages," she conceded.

"Yes; some are not at all clear--even," Mrs. Roby added, "if one is familiar with the original."

"As I suppose you are?" Osric Dane interposed, suddenly fixing her with a look of challenge.

Mrs. Roby met it by a deprecating gesture. "Oh, it's really not difficult up to a certain point; though some of the branches are very little known, and it's almost impossible to get at the source."

"Have you ever tried?" Mrs. Plinth enquired, still distrustful of Mrs. Roby's thoroughness.

Mrs. Roby was silent for a moment; then she replied with lowered lids:

"No--but a friend of mine did; a very brilliant man; and he told me it was best for women--not to...."

A shudder ran around the room. Mrs. Leveret coughed so that the parlour-maid, who was handing the cigarettes, should not hear; Miss Van Vluyck's face took on a nauseated expression, and Mrs. Plinth looked as if she were passing some one she did not care to bow to. But the most remarkable result of Mrs. Roby's words was the effect they produced on the Lunch Club's distinguished guest. Osric Dane's impassive features suddenly softened to an expression of the warmest human sympathy, and edging her chair toward Mrs. Roby's she asked: "Did he really? And--did you find he was right?"

Mrs. Ballinger, in whom annoyance at Mrs. Roby's unwonted assumption of prominence was beginning to displace gratitude for the aid she had rendered, could not consent to her being allowed, by such dubious means, to monopolise the attention of their guest. If Osric Dane had not enough self-respect to resent Mrs. Roby's flippancy, at least the Lunch Club would do so in the person of its President.

Mrs. Ballinger laid her hand on Mrs. Roby's arm. "We must not forget," she said with a frigid amiability, "that absorbing as Xingu is to *us*, it may be less interesting to--"

"Oh, no, on the contrary, I assure you," Osric Dane intervened.

"--to others," Mrs. Ballinger finished firmly; "and we must not allow our little meeting to end without persuading Mrs. Dane to say a few words to us on a subject which, to-day, is much more present in all our thoughts. I refer, of course, to 'The Wings of Death.'"

The other members, animated by various degrees of the same sentiment, and encouraged by the humanised mien of their redoubtable guest, repeated after Mrs. Ballinger: "Oh, yes, you really *must* talk to us a little about your book."

Osric Dane's expression became as bored, though not as haughty, as when her work had been previously mentioned. But before she could respond to Mrs. Ballinger's request, Mrs. Roby had risen from her seat, and was pulling down her veil over her frivolous nose.

"I'm so sorry," she said, advancing toward her hostess with outstretched hand, "but before Mrs. Dane begins I think I'd better run away. Unluckily, as you know, I haven't read her books, so I should be at a terrible disadvantage among you all, and besides, I've an engagement to play bridge."

If Mrs. Roby had simply pleaded her ignorance of Osric Dane's works as a reason for withdrawing, the Lunch Club, in view of her recent prowess, might have approved such evidence of discretion; but to couple this excuse with the brazen announcement that she was foregoing the privilege for the purpose of joining a bridge-party was only one more instance of her deplorable lack of discrimination.

The ladies were disposed, however, to feel that her departure--now that she had performed the sole service she was ever likely to render them--would probably make for greater order and dignity in the impending discussion, besides relieving them of the sense of self-distrust which her presence always mysteriously produced. Mrs. Ballinger therefore restricted herself to a formal murmur of regret, and the other members were just grouping themselves comfortably about Osric Dane when the latter, to their dismay, started up from the sofa on which she had been seated.

"Oh wait--do wait, and I'll go with you!" she called out to Mrs. Roby; and, seizing the hands of the disconcerted members, she administered a series of farewell pressures with the mechanical haste of a railway-conductor punching tickets.

"I'm so sorry--I'd quite forgotten--" she flung back at them from the threshold; and as she joined Mrs. Roby, who had turned in surprise at her appeal, the other ladies had the mortification of hearing her say, in a voice which she did not take the pains to lower: "If you'll let me walk a little way with you, I should so like to ask you a few more questions about Xingu...."

Vikk Simmons

Part 3

The incident had been so rapid that the door closed on the departing pair before the other members had time to understand what was happening. Then a sense of the indignity put upon them by Osric Dane's unceremonious desertion began to contend with the confused feeling that they had been cheated out of their due without exactly knowing how or why.

There was a silence, during which Mrs. Ballinger, with a perfunctory hand, rearranged the skillfully grouped literature at which her distinguished guest had not so much as glanced; then Miss Van Vluyck tartly pronounced: "Well, I can't say that I consider Osric Dane's departure a great loss."

This confession crystallised the resentment of the other members, and Mrs. Leveret exclaimed: "I do believe she came on purpose to be nasty!"

It was Mrs. Plinth's private opinion that Osric Dane's attitude toward the Lunch Club might have been very different had it welcomed her in the majestic setting of the Plinth drawing-rooms; but not liking to reflect on the inadequacy of Mrs. Ballinger's establishment she sought a roundabout satisfaction in depreciating her lack of foresight.

"I said from the first that we ought to have had a subject ready. It's what always happens when you're unprepared. Now if we'd only got up Xingu--"

The slowness of Mrs. Plinth's mental processes was always allowed for by the club; but this instance of it was too much for Mrs. Ballinger's equanimity.

"Xingu!" she scoffed. "Why, it was the fact of our knowing so much more about it than she did--unprepared though we were--

that made Osric Dane so furious. I should have thought that was plain enough to everybody!"

This retort impressed even Mrs. Plinth, and Laura Glyde, moved by an impulse of generosity, said: "Yes, we really ought to be grateful to Mrs. Roby for introducing the topic. It may have made Osric Dane furious, but at least it made her civil."

"I am glad we were able to show her," added Miss Van Vluyck, "that a broad and up-to-date culture is not confined to the great intellectual centres."

This increased the satisfaction of the other members, and they began to forget their wrath against Osric Dane in the pleasure of having contributed to her discomfiture.

Miss Van Vluyck thoughtfully rubbed her spectacles. "What surprised me most," she continued, "was that Fanny Roby should be so up on Xingu."

This remark threw a slight chill on the company, but Mrs. Ballinger said with an air of indulgent irony: "Mrs. Roby always has the knack of making a little go a long way; still, we certainly owe her a debt for happening to remember that she'd heard of Xingu." And this was felt by the other members to be a graceful way of cancelling once for all the club's obligation to Mrs. Roby.

Even Mrs. Leveret took courage to speed a timid shaft of irony. "I fancy Osric Dane hardly expected to take a lesson in Xingu at Hillbridge!"

Mrs. Ballinger smiled. "When she asked me what we represented--do you remember?--I wish I'd simply said we represented Xingu!"

All the ladies laughed appreciatively at this sally, except Mrs. Plinth, who said, after a moment's deliberation: "I'm not sure it would have been wise to do so."

Mrs. Ballinger, who was already beginning to feel as if she had launched at Osric Dane the retort which had just occurred to her, turned ironically on Mrs. Plinth. "May I ask why?" she enquired.

Mrs. Plinth looked grave. "Surely," she said, "I understood from Mrs. Roby herself that the subject was one it was as well not to go into too deeply?"

Miss Van Vluyck rejoined with precision: "I think that applied only to an investigation of the origin of the--of the--"; and suddenly she found that her usually accurate memory had failed her. "It's a part of the subject I never studied myself," she concluded.

"Nor I," said Mrs. Ballinger.

Laura Glyde bent toward them with widened eyes. "And yet it seems--doesn't it?--the part that is fullest of an esoteric fascination?"

"I don't know on what you base that," said Miss Van Vluyck argumentatively.

"Well, didn't you notice how intensely interested Osric Dane became as soon as she heard what the brilliant foreigner--he *was* a foreigner, wasn't he?--had told Mrs. Roby about the origin--the origin of the rite--or whatever you call it?"

Mrs. Plinth looked disapproving, and Mrs. Ballinger visibly wavered. Then she said: "It may not be desirable to touch on the--on that part of the subject in general conversation; but, from the importance it evidently has to a woman of Osric Dane's distinction, I feel as if we ought not to be afraid to discuss it among ourselves--without gloves--though with closed doors, if necessary."

"I'm quite of your opinion," Miss Van Vluyck came briskly to her support; "on condition, that is, that all grossness of language is avoided."

"Oh, I'm sure we shall understand without that," Mrs. Leveret tittered; and Laura Glyde added significantly: "I fancy we can read between the lines," while Mrs. Ballinger rose to assure herself that the doors were really closed.

Mrs. Plinth had not yet given her adhesion. "I hardly see," she began, "what benefit is to be derived from investigating such peculiar customs--"

But Mrs. Ballinger's patience had reached the extreme limit of tension. "This at least," she returned; "that we shall not be placed again in the humiliating position of finding ourselves less up on our own subjects than Fanny Roby!"

Even to Mrs. Plinth this argument was conclusive. She peered furtively about the room and lowered her commanding tones to ask: "Have you got a copy?"

"A--a copy?" stammered Mrs. Ballinger. She was aware that the other members were looking at her expectantly, and that this answer was inadequate, so she supported it by asking another question. "A copy of what?"

Her companions bent their expectant gaze on Mrs. Plinth, who, in turn, appeared less sure of herself than usual. "Why, of--of--the book," she explained.

"What book?" snapped Miss Van Vluyck, almost as sharply as Osric Dane.

Mrs. Ballinger looked at Laura Glyde, whose eyes were interrogatively fixed on Mrs. Leveret. The fact of being deferred to was so new to the latter that it filled her with an insane temerity. "Why, Xingu, of course!" she exclaimed.

A profound silence followed this challenge to the resources of Mrs. Ballinger's library, and the latter, after glancing nervously toward the Books of the Day, returned with dignity: "It's not a thing one cares to leave about."

"I should think not!" exclaimed Mrs. Plinth.

"It is a book, then?" said Miss Van Vluyck.

This again threw the company into disarray, and Mrs. Ballinger, with an impatient sigh, rejoined: "Why--there *is* a book--naturally...."

"Then why did Miss Glyde call it a religion?"

Laura Glyde started up. "A religion? I never--"

"Yes, you did," Miss Van Vluyck insisted; "you spoke of rites; and Mrs. Plinth said it was a custom."

Miss Glyde was evidently making a desperate effort to recall her statement; but accuracy of detail was not her strongest point. At length she began in a deep murmur: "Surely they used to do something of the kind at the Eleusinian mysteries--"

"Oh--" said Miss Van Vluyck, on the verge of disapproval; and Mrs. Plinth protested: "I understood there was to be no indelicacy!"

Mrs. Ballinger could not control her irritation. "Really, it is too bad that we should not be able to talk the matter over quietly among ourselves. Personally, I think that if one goes into Xingu at all--"

"Oh, so do I!" cried Miss Glyde.

"And I don't see how one can avoid doing so, if one wishes to keep up with the Thought of the Day--"

Mrs. Leveret uttered an exclamation of relief. "There--that's it!" she interposed.

"What's it?" the President took her up.

"Why--it's a--a Thought: I mean a philosophy."

This seemed to bring a certain relief to Mrs. Ballinger and Laura Glyde, but Miss Van Vluyck said: "Excuse me if I tell you that you're all mistaken. Xingu happens to be a language."

"A language!" the Lunch Club cried.

"Certainly. Don't you remember Fanny Roby's saying that there were several branches, and that some were hard to trace? What could that apply to but dialects?"

Mrs. Ballinger could no longer restrain a contemptuous laugh. "Really, if the Lunch Club has reached such a pass that it has to go to Fanny Roby for instruction on a subject like Xingu, it had almost better cease to exist!"

"It's really her fault for not being clearer," Laura Glyde put in.

"Oh, clearness and Fanny Roby!" Mrs. Ballinger shrugged. "I daresay we shall find she was mistaken on almost every point."

"Why not look it up?" said Mrs. Plinth.

As a rule this recurrent suggestion of Mrs. Plinth's was ignored in the heat of discussion, and only resorted to afterward in the privacy of each member's home. But on the present occasion the desire to ascribe their own confusion of thought to the vague and contradictory nature of Mrs. Roby's statements caused the members of the Lunch Club to utter a collective demand for a book of reference.

At this point the production of her treasured volume gave Mrs. Leveret, for a moment, the unusual experience of occupying the centre front; but she was not able to hold it long, for *Appropriate Allusions* contained no mention of Xingu.

"Oh, that's not the kind of thing we want!" exclaimed Miss Van Vluyck. She cast a disparaging glance over Mrs. Ballinger's assortment of literature, and added impatiently: "Haven't you any useful books?"

"Of course I have," replied Mrs. Ballinger indignantly; "I keep them in my husband's dressing room."

From this region, after some difficulty and delay, the parlourmaid produced the W-Z volume of an Encyclopaedia and, in deference to the fact that the demand for it had come from Miss Van Vluyck, laid the ponderous tome before her.

There was a moment of painful suspense while Miss Van Vluyck rubbed her spectacles, adjusted them, and turned to Z; and a murmur of surprise when she said: "It isn't here."

"I suppose," said Mrs. Plinth, "it's not fit to be put in a book of reference."

"Oh, nonsense!" exclaimed Mrs. Ballinger. "Try X."

Miss Van Vluyck turned back through the volume, peering short-sightedly up and down the pages, till she came to a stop and remained motionless, like a dog on a point.

"Well, have you found it?" Mrs. Ballinger enquired after a considerable delay.

"Yes. I've found it," said Miss Van Vluyck in a queer voice.

Mrs. Plinth hastily interposed: "I beg you won't read it aloud if there's anything offensive."

Miss Van Vluyck, without answering, continued her silent scrutiny.

"Well, what *is* it?" exclaimed Laura Glyde excitedly.

"*Do* tell us!" urged Mrs. Leveret, feeling that she would have something awful to tell her sister.

Miss Van Vluyck pushed the volume aside and turned slowly toward the expectant group.

"It's a river."

"A *river*?"

"Yes: in Brazil. Isn't that where she's been living?"

"Who? Fanny Roby? Oh, but you must be mistaken. You've been reading the wrong thing," Mrs. Ballinger exclaimed, leaning over her to seize the volume.

"It's the only Xingu in the Encyclopaedia; and she *has* been living in Brazil," Miss Van Vluyck persisted.

"Yes: her brother has a consulship there," Mrs. Leveret interposed.

"But it's too ridiculous! I--we--why we *all* remember studying Xingu last year--or the year before last," Mrs. Ballinger stammered.

"I thought I did when *you* said so," Laura Glyde avowed.

"I said so?" cried Mrs. Ballinger.

"Yes. You said it had crowded everything else out of your mind."

"Well *you* said it had changed your whole life!"

"For that matter. Miss Van Vluyck said she had never grudged the time she'd given it."

Mrs. Plinth interposed: "I made it clear that I knew nothing whatever of the original."

Mrs. Ballinger broke off the dispute with a groan. "Oh, what does it all matter if she's been making fools of us? I believe Miss Van Vluyck's right--she was talking of the river all the while!"

"How could she? It's too preposterous," Miss Glyde exclaimed.

"Listen." Miss Van Vluyck had repossessed herself of the Encyclopaedia, and restored her spectacles to a nose reddened by excitement. "'The Xingu, one of the principal rivers of Brazil, rises on the plateau of Mato Grosso, and flows in a northerly direction for a length of no less than one thousand one hundred and eighteen miles, entering the Amazon near the mouth of the latter river. The upper course of the Xingu is auriferous and fed by numerous branches. Its source was first discovered in 1884 by the German explorer von den Steinen, after a difficult and dangerous expedition through a region inhabited by tribes still in the Stone Age of culture.'"

The ladies received this communication in a state of stupefied silence from which Mrs. Leveret was the first to rally. "She certainly *did* speak of its having branches."

The word seemed to snap the last thread of their incredulity. "And of its great length," gasped Mrs. Ballinger.

"She said it was awfully deep, and you couldn't skip--you just had to wade through," Miss Glyde added.

The idea worked its way more slowly through Mrs. Plinth's compact resistances. "How could there be anything improper about a river?" she enquired.

"Improper?"

"Why, what she said about the source--that it was corrupt?"

"Not corrupt, but hard to get at," Laura Glyde corrected. "Some one who'd been there had told her so. I daresay it was the explorer himself--doesn't it say the expedition was dangerous?"

"'Difficult and dangerous,'" read Miss Van Vluyck.

Mrs. Ballinger pressed her hands to her throbbing temples. "There's nothing she said that wouldn't apply to a river--to this river!" She swung about excitedly to the other members. "Why, do you remember her telling us that she hadn't read 'The Supreme Instant' because she'd taken it on a boating party while she was staying with her brother, and some one had 'shied' it overboard--'shied' of course was her own expression."

The ladies breathlessly signified that the expression had not escaped them.

"Well--and then didn't she tell Osric Dane that one of her books was simply saturated with Xingu? Of course it was, if one of Mrs. Roby's rowdy friends had thrown it into the river!"

This surprising reconstruction of the scene in which they had just participated left the members of the Lunch Club inarticulate. At length, Mrs. Plinth, after visibly labouring with the problem, said in a heavy tone: "Osric Dane was taken in too."

Mrs. Leveret took courage at this. "Perhaps that's what Mrs. Roby did it for. She said Osric Dane was a brute, and she may have wanted to give her a lesson."

Miss Van Vluyck frowned. "It was hardly worth while to do it at our expense."

"At least," said Miss Glyde with a touch of bitterness, "she succeeded in interesting her, which was more than we did."

"What chance had we?" rejoined Mrs. Ballinger.

"Mrs. Roby monopolised her from the first. And *that*, I've no doubt, was her purpose--to give Osric Dane a false impression of her own standing in the club. She would hesitate at nothing to attract attention: we all know how she took in poor Professor Foreland."

"She actually makes him give bridge-teas every Thursday," Mrs. Leveret piped up.

Laura Glyde struck her hands together. "Why, this is Thursday, and it's *there* she's gone, of course; and taken Osric with her!"

"And they're shrieking over us at this moment," said Mrs. Ballinger between her teeth.

This possibility seemed too preposterous to be admitted. "She would hardly dare," said Miss Van Vluyck, "confess the imposture to Osric Dane."

"I'm not so sure: I thought I saw her make a sign as she left. If she hadn't made a sign, why should Osric Dane have rushed out after her?"

"Well, you know, we'd all been telling her how wonderful Xingu was, and she said she wanted to find out more about it," Mrs. Leveret said, with a tardy impulse of justice to the absent.

This reminder, far from mitigating the wrath of the other members, gave it a stronger impetus.

"Yes--and that's exactly what they're both laughing over now," said Laura Glyde ironically.

Mrs. Plinth stood up and gathered her expensive furs about her monumental form. "I have no wish to criticise," she said; "but unless the Lunch Club can protect its members against the recurrence of such--such unbecoming scenes, I for one--"

"Oh, so do I!" agreed Miss Glyde, rising also.

Miss Van Vluyck closed the Encyclopaedia and proceeded to button herself into her jacket "My time is really too valuable--" she began.

"I fancy we are all of one mind," said Mrs. Ballinger, looking searchingly at Mrs. Leveret, who looked at the others.

"I always deprecate anything like a scandal--" Mrs. Plinth continued.

"She has been the cause of one today!" exclaimed Miss Glyde.

Mrs. Leveret moaned: "I don't see how she *could*!" and Miss Van Vluyck said, picking up her notebook: "Some women stop at nothing."

"--but if," Mrs. Plinth took up her argument impressively, "anything of the kind had happened in *my* house" (it never would have, her tone implied), "I should have felt that I owed it to myself either to ask for Mrs. Roby's resignation--or to offer mine."

"Oh, Mrs. Plinth--" gasped the Lunch Club.

"Fortunately for me," Mrs. Plinth continued with an awful magnanimity, "the matter was taken out of my hands by our President's decision that the right to entertain distinguished guests was a privilege vested in her office; and I think the other members will agree that, as she was alone in this opinion, she ought to be alone in deciding on the best way of effacing its--its really deplorable consequences."

A deep silence followed this outbreak of Mrs. Plinth's long-stored resentment.

"I don't see why I should be expected to ask her to resign--" Mrs. Ballinger at length began; but Laura Glyde turned back to remind her: "You know she made you say that you'd got on swimmingly in Xingu."

An ill-timed giggle escaped from Mrs. Leveret, and Mrs. Ballinger energetically continued "--but you needn't think for a moment that I'm afraid to!"

The door of the drawing-room closed on the retreating backs of the Lunch Club, and the President of that distinguished association, seating herself at her writing table, and pushing away a copy of "The Wings of Death" to make room for her elbow, drew forth a sheet of the club's note-paper, on which she began to write: "My dear Mrs. Roby--"

The Vice of Reading

That "diffusion of knowledge" commonly classed with steam-heat and universal suffrage in the category of modern improvements, has incidentally brought about the production of a new vice -- the vice of reading.

No vices are so hard to eradicate as those which are popularly regarded as virtues. Among these the vice of reading is foremost. That reading trash is a vice is generally conceded; but reading *per se*-- the habit of reading -- new as it is, already ranks with such seasoned virtues as thrift, sobriety, early rising and regular exercise. There is, indeed, something peculiarly aggressive in the virtuousness of the sense-of-duty reader. By those who have kept to the humble paths of precept he is revered as following a counsel of perfection. "I wish I had kept up my reading as you have," the unlettered novice declares to this adept in the supererogatory; and the reader, accustomed to the incense of uncritical applause, not unnaturally looks on his occupation as a noteworthy intellectual achievement.

Reading deliberately undertaken -- what may be called volitional reading -- is no more reading than erudition is culture. Real reading is reflex action; the born reader reads as unconsciously as he breathes; and, to carry the analogy a degree farther, reading is no more a virtue than breathing. Just in proportion as it is considered meritorious does it become unprofitable. What is reading, in the last analysis, but an interchange of thought between writer and reader? If the book enters the reader's mind just as it left the writer's -- without any of the additions and modifications inevitably produced by contact with a new body of thought -- it has been read to no purpose. In such cases, of course, the reader is not always to blame. There are books that are always the same -- incapable of modifying or of being modified -- but these do not count as factors in literature. The value of books is proportionate to what may be called their plasticity -- their quality of being all things to all men, of being diversely molded by the impact of fresh forms of thought. Where, from one cause or the other, this reciprocal adaptability is lacking, there can be no real intercourse between book and reader. In this sense it may be said that there is no abstract standard of values in literature: the greatest books ever written are worth to each reader only what he can get out of them. The best books are those from which the best readers have been able to extract the greatest amount of thought of the highest quality; but it is generally from these books that the poor reader gets least.

To be a poor reader may therefore be considered a misfortune; but it is certainly not a fault. Why should we all be readers? We are not all expected to be musicians; but read we must; and so those that cannot read creatively read mechanically -- as though a man who had no aptitude for the violin were to regard the grinding of a barrel-organ as an equivalent accomplishment! It must be understood at the outset that, in the matter of reading, the real offenders are not those who restrict themselves to recognized trash. There is little harm in the self-confessed devourer of foolish fiction. He who feasts upon "the novel of the day" does not seriously impede the development of literature. The cast of mind which discerns in the natural divisions of the melon an indication that it is meant to be eaten *en faille*, might even look upon certain works -- the penny-in-the-slot or touch-the-button books, which require no effort beyond turning the pages and using one's eyes -- as especially designed for the consumption of the mechanical reader. Providence turns out an unfailing supply of authors whose obvious mission it is thus to protect literature from the ravages of the unintelligent; and it is only when he strays from his predestined pastures that the mechanical reader becomes a danger to the body of letters. The idea that reading is a moral quality has unhappily led many conscientious persons to renounce their innocuous dalliance with light literature for more strenuous intercourse. These are the persons who "make it a rule to read." The "platform" of the more ambitious actually includes the large resolve to keep up with all that is being written! The desire to keep up is apparently the strongest incentive to this class of readers: they seem to regard literature as a cable-car that can be "boarded" only by running; while many a born reader may be found unblushingly loitering in the tea-cup times of stage-coach and posting-chaise, without so much as being aware of the new means of locomotion.

It is when the mechanical reader, armed with this high conception of his duty, invades the domain of letters -- discusses, criticizes, condemns, or, worse still, praises -- that the vice of reading becomes a menace to literature. Even so, it might seem in questionable taste to resent an intrusion prompted by motives so respectable, were it not that the incorrigible self-sufficiency of the mechanical reader makes him a fair object of attack. The man who grinds the barrel-organ does not challenge comparison with Paderewski, but the mechanical reader never doubts his intellectual competency. As grace gives faith, so zeal for self-improvement is supposed to confer brains.

To read is not a virtue; but to read well is an art, and an art that only the born reader can acquire. The gift of reading is no exception to the rule that all natural gifts need to be cultivated by practice and discipline; but unless the innate aptitude exists the training will be wasted. It is the delusion of the mechanical reader to think that intentions may take the place of aptitude.

So far is this from being the case that there are certain generic signs by which the born reader detects his manufactured copy under whatever guise the latter may assume. One of these idiosyncrasies is the habit of regarding reading objectively. The mechanical reader, as he always reads consciously, knows exactly how much he reads, and will tell you so with the pride of the careful housekeeper who has calculated to within half an ounce the daily consumption of food in her household. As the housekeeper is apt to go to market every day at a certain hour, so the mechanical reader has often a fixed time for laying in his intellectual stores; and not infrequently he reads for just so many hours a day. The statement in one of Hamerton's youthful diaries -- "I shall now commence a course of poetical reading, beginning with 50 hours of Chaucer, and as I gave him 1 1/2 last night it leaves me exactly 48 1/2" -- is a good example of this kind of reading. It follows that he who reads by time often "has no time to read"; a plight unknown to the born reader, whose reading forms a continuous undercurrent to all his other occupations.

The mechanical reader is the slave of his book-mark: if he lose his place he is under the irksome necessity of beginning again at the beginning; and a story is told of one such reader whom a flippant relative kept for a year at "Fire and Sword in the Soudan" by the unfeeling stratagem of shifting the marker every night. The born reader is his own book-mark. He instinctively remembers at what stage in the argument he laid his book down, and the pages open of themselves at the point for which he is looking. It is due to the mechanical reader to say that he is uniformly scrupulous in the performance of his task: it is one of his rules never to skip a word, and he can always meet with a triumphant affirmative Dr. Johnson's immortal "Do you read books through?" This inexorable principle is doubtless based on the fact that the mechanical reader is incapable of discerning intuitively whether a book is worth reading or not. In fact, until he has read the last line of a book he is unable to form any opinion of it; nor can he give any adequate reasons for his opinion when formed. Viewing all books from the outside, and having no point of contact with the author's mind, he makes no allowances for temperament or environment; for that process of transposition and selection that makes the most impersonal book the product of unique conditions.

It is obvious that the mechanical reader, taking each book separately as an entity suspended in the inane, must miss all the by-paths and cross-cuts of his subject. He is like a tourist who drives from one "sight" to another without looking at anything that is not set down in Baedeker. Of the delights of intellectual vagrancy, of the improvised chase after a fleeting allusion, suggested sometimes by the turn of a phrase or by the mere complexion of a word, he is serenely unaware. With him the book's the thing: the idea of using it as the keynote of unpremeditated harmonies, as the gateway into some *paysage choisi* of the spirit, is beyond his ken.

The mechanical reader considers it his duty to read every book that is talked about; a duty rendered less onerous by the fact that he can judge beforehand, from the material dimensions of each book, how much space it will take up in his head: there is no need to allow for expansion. To the mechanical reader, books once read are not like growing things that strike root and intertwine branches, but like fossils ticketed and put away in the drawers of a geologist's cabinet; or rather, like prisoners condemned to lifelong solitary confinement. In such a mind the books never talk to each other.

The course of the mechanical reader is guided by the *vox populi*. He makes straight for the book that is being talked about, and his sense of its importance is in proportion to the number of editions exhausted before publication, since he has no means of distinguishing between the different classes of books talked about, nor between the voices that do the talking. It is a part of the whole duty of the mechanical reader to pronounce an opinion on every book he reads, and he is sometimes driven to strange shifts in the conscientious performance of this task. It is his nature to mistrust and dislike every book he does not understand. "I cannot read and therefore wish all books burned." In his heart of hearts the mechanical reader may sometimes echo this wish of Envy in Doctor Faustus; but, it being also a part of his duty to be "fond of reading," he is obliged to repress his bibliocidal impulse, and go through the form of trying the case, when lynching would have been so much simpler.

It is only natural that the reader who looks on reading as a moral obligation should confound moral and intellectual judgments. Here is a book that every one is talking about; the number of its editions is an almost unanswerable proof of its merit; but to the mechanical reader it is cryptic, and he takes refuge in disapproval. He admits the cleverness, of course; but one of the characters is "not nice"; ergo, the book is not nice; he is surprised that you should have cared to read it. The mechanical reader, after a few such experiments, learns the potency of disapproval as a critical weapon, and it soon becomes his chief defence against the irritating demand to admire what he cannot understand. Sometimes his disapprobation is tempered by philosophic concessions to human laxity: as in the case of the lady who could not approve of Balzac's novels, but was of course willing to admit that "they were written in the most beautiful French." A fine instance of this temperate disapproval is furnished by Mrs. Barbauld's verdict upon The Ancient Mariner: she "pronounced it improbable."

The obligation of expressing an opinion on every book which is being talked about has led to the reprehensible but natural habit of borrowing opinions. Any one who frequents a group of mechanical readers soon becomes accustomed to their socialistic use of certain formulas, and to the rapid process of erosion and distortion undergone by much-borrowed opinions. There have been known persons heartless enough to find pleasure in taking the mechanical reader unawares with the demand for an opinion; and it must be owned that the result sometimes justifies the theory that no sports are so diverting as those which are seasoned with cruelty. In such extremities, the expedients resorted to by mechanical readers often do justice to their inventiveness; as when a lady, on being suddenly asked what she thought of "Quo Vadis," replied that she had no fault to find with the book except that "nothing happened in it."

Thus far the subject has dealt only with what may be called the average mechanical reader: a designation embracing the immense majority of book-consumers. There is, however, another and more striking type of mechanical reader -- he who, wearying of the Philistine diversion of "understanding the obvious," boldly threads his way "amid the bitterness of things occult." Transcendentalism owes much of its perennial popularity to a reverence for the unintelligible, and its disciples are largely recruited from the class of readers who consider it as great an intellectual feat to read a book as to understand it. But these votaries of the esoteric are too few in number to be harmful. It is the average mechanical reader who really endangers the integrity of letters; this may seem a curious charge to bring against that voracious majority. How can those who create the demand for the hundredth thousand be accused of malice toward letters?

In that acute character-study, "Manoeuvring," Miss Edgeworth says of one of her characters: "Her mind had never been overwhelmed by a torrent of wasteful learning. That the stream of literature had passed over it was apparent only from its fertility." There could hardly be a happier description of those who read intuitively; and its antithesis as fitly portrays the mechanical reader. His mind is devastated by that torrent of wasteful learning which his demands have helped to swell. It is probable that if no one read but those who know how to read, none would produce books but those who know how to write; but it is the least offence of the mechanical reader to have encouraged the mechanical author. The two were made for each other and may prey on one another with impunity.

The harmfulness of the mechanical reader is fourfold. In the first place, by bringing about the demand for mediocre writing, he facilitates the career of the mediocre author. The crime of luring creative talent into the ranks of mechanical production is in fact the gravest offence of the mechanical reader.

Secondly, by his passion for "popular" renderings of abstruse and difficult subjects, by confounding the hastiest *rechauffe* of scientific truisms with the slowly-matured conceptions of the original thinker, he retards true culture and lessens the possible amount of really abiding work.

The habit of confusing moral and intellectual judgments is the third cause of his harmfulness to literature. The inadequacy of "art for art's sake" as a literary creed has long been conceded. It is not by requiring that the imaginative writer shall be touched "to fine issues" that the mechanical reader interferes with the production of masterpieces, but by his own inability to discern the "fine issues" of any book, however great, which presents some incidental stumbling-block to his vision. To those who regard literature as a criticism of life, nothing is more puzzling than this incapacity to distinguish between the general tendency of a book -- its technical and imaginative value as a whole -- and its merely episodical features. That the mechanical reader should confound the unmoral with the immoral is perhaps natural; he may be pardoned for an erroneous classification of such books as "La Chartreuse de Parma" or the "Life of Benevento Cellini"; his harmfulness to literature lies in his persistent ignorance of the fact that any serious portrayal of life must be judged not by the incidents it presents but by the author's sense of their significance. The harmful book is the trivial book: it depends on the writer, and not on the subject, whether the contemplation of life results in Faust or Fibulas. To gauge the absence of this perception in the average reader, one must turn to the ordinary "improper" book of current English and American fiction. In these works, enjoyed under protest, with the plea that they are "unpleasant, but so powerful," one sees the reflection of the image which the great portrayals of life leave on the minds of the mechanical reader and his novelist. There is the collocation of "painful" incidents; but the rest, being unperceived, is left out.

Finally, the mechanical reader, by his demand for patronized literature, and his inability to distinguish between the means and the end, has misdirected the tendencies of criticism, or rather, has produced a creature in his own image -- the mechanical critic. The London correspondent of a New York paper recently quoted a "well-known English reviewer" as saying that people no longer had time to read critical analyses of books -- that what they wanted was a resume of the contents. It is of course an open question (and hardly within the scope of this argument) how much literature is benefited by criticism; but to speak as though the analysis of a book were one kind of criticism and the cataloguing of its contents another, is a manifest absurdity. The born reader may or may not wish to hear what the critics have to say of a book; but if he cares for any criticism he wants the only kind worthy of the name -- an analysis of subject and manner. He who has no time for such criticism will certainly spare none to the summing-up of the contents of a book: an inventory of its incidents, ending up with the conventional "But we will not spoil the reader's enjoyment by revealing, etc." It is the mechanical reader who demands such inventories and calls them criticisms; and it is because the mechanical reader is in the majority that the mechanical plot-extractor is fast superseding the critic. Whether real criticism be of service to literature or not, it is clear that this pseudo-reviewing is harmful, since it places books of very different qualities on the same dead level of mediocrity, by ignoring their true purport and significance. It is impossible to give an idea of the value of any book, except perhaps a detective-story, by the recapitulation of its contents; and even those qualities which differentiate the good from the bad detective-story lie not so much in the collocation of incidents as in the handling of the subject and the choice of means used for producing a given effect. All forms of art are based on the principle of selection, and where that principle is held of no account in the sum-total of any intellectual production; there can be no genuine criticism.

It is thus that the mechanical reader systematically works against the best in literature. Obviously, it is to the writer that he is most harmful. The broad way that leads to his approval is so easy to tread and so thronged with prosperous fellow-travelers that many a young pilgrim has been drawn into it by the mere craving for companionship; and perhaps it is not until the journey's end, when he reaches the Palace of Platitudes and sits down to a feast of indiscriminate praise, with the scribblers he has most despised helping themselves unreported out of the very dish prepared in his honor, that his thoughts turn longingly to that other way -- the strait path leading "To The Happy Few."

Edith Wharton, 1903

Reader Discussion Guide

Enter the Witty World of Wharton

Why read Edith Wharton? Isn't she one of those stuffy, classical writers that modern readers shy away from? I don't know about stuffy, but given that she was the first woman to win the Pulitzer Prize, Wharton is one of America's great novelists, and her works are considered classics. In the short story *Xingu*, Wharton brings her immense talent to bear on a tale that displays her wit, sarcasm, and renowned gift for irony. *Xingu* is short and funny. Wharton is delightful as she plays with the characters and surprises readers with jokes, puns, and wordplay.

Xingu is a fun tale that is perfect for anyone who loves books, enjoys reading, and discussing books. Wharton's satirical look at what happens during a women's lunch club achieves perfect pitch. No character is left untouched. The reader is joyously led through the tale with the ladies of the reading group as they work to impress a popular visiting novelist and divine the true nature of *Xingu*. In the end, the reader is delighted with the twists and turns that inevitably lead to a big surprise.

Wharton wrote this short tale in 1911 around the time when Henry James had begun work on his autobiography. The two writers were good friends. Because James had a brother who had traveled to Brazil, it's assumed that Wharton learned of the Amazon tributary known as Xingu from James.

Wharton's ideas about readers and reading were well known by then. She had published her essay *The Vice of Reading* in

1903 where she discussed readers she labeled "mechanical readers," those who consume books the way department store shoppers consumed the many products lining the shelves.

Just as there's been an increase in book clubs and reading discussion groups today, similar book clubs were the rage in Wharton's time. Women gathered to discuss the good books of the day and, when possible, to talk and listen to authors.

Somehow, these three separate elements combined and informed the creation of Wharton's fun tale, *Xingu*.

Discussion Questions

You may have chosen this particular edition of *Xingu* for a variety of reasons. The following questions are food for thought for you or a book club.

- Edith Wharton loved to examine how society impacts lives. Is there a certain sense of hierarchy among the women in the book club? Did that feed into the story?
- Would you consider this short story to be a work of manners? If so, in what way? If not, why not?
- Why do you think the ladies acted the way they did once Mrs. Roby introduced the topic of Xingu? Have you seen this type of behavior before?
- What did you notice about the ways the ladies reacted to the famous novelist in their midst? Do you think people today react in similar ways to celebrities?
- Why do you think the ladies acted the way they did? Were they trying to impress Osric Dane?
- What did you think about Mrs. Roby at the beginning of the story? Did your reaction to her change? When?
- How do you think you would have reacted had you been a member of the Lunch Club?
- Do you think Wharton tried to manipulate the way the reader thinks about the various ladies of the Lunch Club? How?

Prefer an audio version? Go to this link and scroll down:

http://bit.ly/xinguaudio

Vikk Simmons

Quotes from Xingu

"Mrs. Ballinger is one of the ladies who pursue Culture in bands, as though it were dangerous to meet alone. To this end she had founded the Lunch Club, an association composed of herself and several other indomitable huntresses of erudition."
(Edith Wharton, Xingu)

"I suppose she flattered him," Miss Van Vluyck summed up--"or else it's the way she does her hair." (Edith Wharton, Xingu)

"Amusement," said Mrs. Plinth, "is hardly what I look for in my choice of books." (Edith Wharton, Xingu)

"It was only the fact of having a dull sister who thought her clever that saved her from a sense of hopeless inferiority."
(Edith Wharton, Xingu)

"Books were written to read; if one read them, what more could be expected? To be questioned in detail regarding the contents of a volume seemed to her as great an outrage as being searched for smuggled laces at the Custom House." (Edith Wharton, Xingu)

"Her mind was a hotel where facts came and went like transient lodgers, without leaving their address behind, and frequently without paying for their board." (Edith Wharton, Xingu)

Vikk Simmons

Who is Edith Wharton?

Edith Wharton, the famous novelist, was born Edith Newbold Jones. A true little girl of the ages, when asked what she wanted to be when she grew up, she stated: "The best-dressed woman in New York." Painfully shy, young Edith could not have been thrilled to have been blessed with a head of look-at-me red hair.

Young Edith had the run of her father's library. Instead of the books written for children like the ones offered to kids today, Edith read the great works of history and philosophy, poetry and works by Goethe. She was an imaginative child, too. Wharton, herself, would say that as a young child "she had the habit of making things up."

Edith Wharton, the Writer

Wharton was a prolific writer. In addition to the novels that brought her great fame, she also published short stories and nonfiction. Her nonfiction included works on travel, interior design, and gardening.

As a young girl, Wharton would write her stories on wrapping paper. Paper, after all, was way too expensive to waste on a child's scribbling. Despite her fame as a novelist today, young Edith only wrote one novel as a child at the tender age of eleven. Her mother's cold criticism dampened the creative flame, and so the budding writer turned to poetry for some time afterwards.

Vikk Simmons

Edith Wharton and Film

Obviously Wharton didn't write for the cinema, but that didn't stop directors from turning her works into movies. *The House of Mirth* became a silent film in 1918 and, in 2000, director Terence Davies turned to Wharton's famous novel to produce another film adaption for today's movie-goers. Directors such as Martin Scorsese and Robert Allan Ackerman have released film adaptations of Wharton's work. Bette Davis and Joan Crawford starred in cinema versions. You'll even find a TV adaptation of *The House of Mirth* from the 1980s.

Edith Wharton and Henry James

If there was one writer Edith Wharton admired, it was certainly Henry James. It may have been the 1890s, but Edith Wharton pursued the older novelist. She determined they would be friends. The two were a most unlikely pair. He grew up in Europe and lived in England; she came from the wealthy society of old New York.

Though they may have been friends, the two didn't always see eye-to-eye when it came to the other's work. When Henry James made some veiled remarks in one of his novels that cast a negative tone on Wharton's work, she didn't take it lightly. Many believe that the title for Osric Dane's novel, *Wings Over Death*, is a play on James's novel *Wings Over Doves*.

Writings by Edith Wharton

As mentioned earlier, Wharton was a prolific writer. She wrote both fiction and nonfiction and loved to write about things that interested her. That's why you'll find essays, design books, books on houses and gardens, travel books, and a book on writing, as well as novels, novellas, and short stories. She wrote 38 novels and novellas, and well over 85 short stories. Although she wrote her first novel at the age of eleven, her mother's cold reception dampened her enthusiasm. In later years, many adored Wharton's novel *Ethan Frome*, but she won the Pulitzer Prize for *The Age of Innocence*. Even today, her novel *The House of Mirth* continues to draw readers.

Wharton drew on her own history to offer accurate portrayals of New England and Old New York. Her work often has a strong current of dramatic irony. Many of her novels focus on marriage, the state of women, class struggles, and the clash of old wealth versus new. Yet she was not afraid to venture out, and her ghost stories continue to be popular and draw new readers.

The Edith Wharton - Lily Elsie Connection

The Edwardian beauty Lily Elsie, the most photographed woman of her day, graces the cover.

I confess, I did not find a direct connection between Edith Wharton and Lily Elsie, the woman featured on the cover. Still, Lily Elsie, a popular English actress and singer, may well have crossed paths with Edith Wharton. Although I could not find any documentation that the two women met, Wharton visited England many times. I don't think it's out of the realm of possibility that they may have met.

This particular portrait of Lily Elsie captures the look and the promise of Wharton's women, and I can imagine Lily Elsie, book in hand, chatting away with the Ladies Lunch Club women -- and what a tale that would be.

I did find one slim connection between the two women. While Lily Elsie is usually remembered as the star of *The Merry Widow*, she also starred in the popular 1909 premiere of the English-speaking *The Dollar Princess* produced the same year she sat for the cover photograph. The term "dollar princess" had become a nickname given to the American heiresses who flooded Europe in search of royal marriages. In fact, Edith Wharton's cousin, Anita Rhinelander Stewart, became known as the first true Dollar Princess when, in 1909, she married Dom Miguel of Braganza, Infant of Portugal, Duke of Viseu.

Like many royals of his day, the Prince of Braganza was in need of funds and had been intent on marrying an heiress, a *royal* heiress. Instead he proposed to Ms. Rhinelander, an American heiress and no royal. They were married three months after they met. Some have said Anita Rhinelander was made a royal princess the day before her marriage by the Austrian Emperor Franz Joseph, but this has been disputed by

Marlene Eilers Koenig. It seems Ms Rhinelander's mother agreed to "hand over" a million dollars to the good prince the day he married her daughter. In case you're wondering, according to Marlene Eilers Koenig, that would be worth more than 21 million dollars today.

In her last novel, *The Buccaneers,* Wharton spins a tale of three dollar princesses. While Wharton died before she could complete this novel, fifty years later Marion Mainwaring, a Wharton scholar, completed the novel, and it is still available.

The Downtown Abbey Connection

Fans of Downtown Abbey are familiar with dollar princesses. Cora Crawley is the show's dollar princess. Crawley, a rich American, marries an Earl. Many of the themes explored on Downtown Abbey are at the heart of Wharton's work.

Conclusion

I hope you enjoyed reading Edith Wharton's short story *Xingu* and found it as delightful as I have. I'm discovering Edith Wharton to be a fascinating writer and find that I'm being drawn to read more and more of her work. She captures the Edwardian age so well, and she's become the Pied Piper of the age, drawing me further and further into that time. Perhaps, like me, you'll pick up the same trail left by Wharton. I hope so.

If you do, or if you'd like to share your own thoughts on *Xingu, The Vice of Reading* essay, Edith Wharton, or even Lily Elsie, please feel free to write me:

DownTheWritersPath@gmail.com

I'd love to hear from you. You can also visit my blog, Down the Writer's Path:

DownTheWritersPath.com

One of the fun things about doing a book like this is making discoveries along the way. I found that Lily Elsie, the woman featured on the cover, and I share the same birthday. Edith Wharton's cousin was born on the same day that my parents married. Lily Elsie starred in The Dollar Princess in 1909, and Wharton's cousin married her prince the same year. I stumbled across Lily Elsie's photograph the same way I happily discovered Wharton's essay on reading. While these aren't of any real importance, for me, they're happy connections that breathed energy into my creative process. That's part of the fun of reading, and sharing Xingu with you is part of the fun of writing. I hope you've enjoyed your time here and will share this book with others.

Don't forget to read Wharton's essay, *The Vice of Reading.*

Vikk Simmons, 2014

Postscript

Thank you for purchasing this book! If you enjoyed this book, please take a moment to share your thoughts and post a review. It would be greatly appreciated.

Prefer an audio version? Go to this link and scroll down:

http://bit.ly/xinguaudio

Appendix A

Short Stories by Edith Wharton

Edith Wharton wrote about what she knew. While Wharton used the Old New York setting for much of her work, at least a third is in New England. She delved deeply into the behaviors of the old guard high society and their clash with the "new" wealthy. She wrote of fashion, of marriage and divorce, of artists and their struggles. Her insight and ability to capture the inner lives of her characters is well known.

Mrs. Manstey's View

The Fullness of Life

The Lamp of Psyche

That Good May Come

The Valley of Childish Things, and Other Emblems

The Greater Inclination

The Muse's Tragedy

A Journey

The Pelican

Souls Belated

A Coward

The Twilight of the God

A Cup of Cold Water

The Portrait

April Showers

Friends

The Line of Least Resistance

The Duchess at Prayer

The Angel at the Grave

The Recovery

Copy: A Dialogue

The Rembrandt

The Moving Finger

The Confessional

The Descent of Man

The Mission of Jane

The Other Two

The Quicksand

The Dilettante

The Reckoning

Expiation

The Lady's Maid's Bell

A Venetian Night's Entertainment

The Letter

The House of the Dead Hand

The Introducers

Les Metteurs en Scene

The Hermit and the Wild Woman

The Last Asset

In Trust

The Pretext

The Verdict

The Pot-Boiler

The Best Man

The Bolted Door

His Father's Son

The Daunt Diana

The Debt

Full Circle

The Legend

The Eyes

The Blond Beast

Afterward

The Letters

The Greater Inclination

The Touchstone

Xingu

Coming Home

Autre Temps

Kerfol

The Long Run

The Triumph of Night

The Choice

Bunner Sisters

Writing a War Story

Miss Mary Pask

The Young Gentlemen

Bewitched

The Seed of the Faith

The Temperate Zone

Velvet Ear Pads

Atrophy

A Bottle of Perrier

After Holbein

Dieu d'Amour

The Refugees

Mr. Jones

Her Son

The Day of the Funeral

A Glimpse

Joy in the House

Diagnosis

Charm Incorporated

Pomegranate Seed

Confession

Roman Fever

The Looking Glass

Duration

All Souls

About Vikk Simmons

Vikk Simmons has been reading the classics since she was a young girl who eagerly waited for the monthly Heritage Press editions. She's convinced that her bibliophile tendencies were stirred as she opened those books and read the accompanying pamphlets called The Sandglass. Each Heritage Press Sandglass would provide extensive information on the author and how that particular work developed. In addition, wonderful information about the design of the book would be discussed from type to paper to the selection of fonts. Information about the illustrations and the illustrator's history and philosophy. would be discussed. It was an exciting time to read.

She is also a writer, an avid journaler, and the creator of the Coffee Break Journals. (CoffeeBreakJournals.com)

COFFEE BREAK JOURNALS

Discover Coffee Break Journals and journaling, be sure and get your free copy of *Why Writers Keep Journals*:

CoffeeBreakJournals.com

The COFFEE BREAK JOURNAL
for FICTION WRITERS

The COFFEE BREAK JOURNAL
for NONFICTION WRITERS

The COFFEE BREAK JOURNAL
for CREATIVE WRITERS

The COFFEE BREAK JOURNAL
for ROMANCE WRITERS

The COFFEE BREAK JOURNAL *for* TEEN WRITERS

The COFEE BREAK JOURNAL *for* POETS

Vikk Simmons is a writer and a lifelong journaler. She has an MFA in Creative Writing from Vermont College and has taught writing and facilitated Artist Way groups for many years. She has been certified since 1998 to teach the acclaimed *Journal to the Self* program developed by Kay Adams.

Coffee Break Journals are developed by Vikk Simmons to encourage people from all walks of life to discover, explore, and enjoy the many rewards of journal writing.

Printed in Great Britain
by Amazon

65980527R00050